SHREDDERMAN

SHREDDERMAN
ENEMY SPY

bY: WENdELiN VaN DraaNEN

iLLUSTraTeD BY: BriaN BiGGS

Alfred A. Knopf
New York

THIS IS A BORZOI BOOK PUBLISHED BY ALFRED A. KNOPF

Text copyright © 2005 by Wendelin Van Draanen Parsons
Illustrations copyright © 2005 by Brian Biggs
All rights reserved under International and Pan-American Copyright
Conventions. Published in the United States by Alfred A. Knopf, an imprint of
Random House Children's Books, a division of Random House, Inc., New York,
and simultaneously in Canada by Random House of Canada Limited, Toronto.
Distributed by Random House, Inc., New York.
KNOPF, BORZOI BOOKS, and the colophon are registered trademarks of
Random House, Inc.

www.randomhouse.com/kids

Library of Congress Cataloging-in-Publication Data
Van Draanen, Wendelin.
Enemy spy / by Wendelin Van Draanen ; illustrated by Brian Biggs. — 1st ed.
p.   cm. — (Shredderman ; 4)
SUMMARY: When Nolan witnesses a serious crime, he realizes he may not be able
to hide behind his Shredderman identity this time.
ISBN 0-375-82354-9 (trade) — ISBN 0-375-92354-3 (lib. bdg.)
[1. Heroes—Fiction. 2. Spies—Fiction. 3. Schools—Fiction.] I. Biggs, Brian, ill.
II. Title.
PZ7.D779En   2005
[Fic]—dc22   2004026926

Printed in the United States of America
May 2005
10 9 8 7 6 5 4 3 2 1
First Edition

WENdELiN VAN DrAANEN

For my shreddin' nieces, Hilary, Lauren, Molly, and Shelby.
And special thanks to TV news anchor Wendy Thies for her
help with research. (So glad you're not like Chatty!)

BriaN BiGGS

For Laurie, David, and Erin.

CONTENTS

CHAPTER 1
The Trouble Begins

I knew I was in trouble when they showed my Web site on the evening news. It wasn't just the local news, either. It was *national* news.

All of a sudden, Shredderman—uh, that would be *me* as a mighty-muscled superhero—flew across the TV screen in a mask and a purple cape.

Then the *shredderman.com* banner fluttered onto the screen and my sidekick, the Bouncer—who is really, *shhhhh*, Mr. Green, my *teacher*—flexed his muscles and rocked out to the Shredderman theme song.

Brrong . . . b-brong . . . br-br-br-br-br-br-br-brong.

Mr. Green can really shred on guitar!

The newscaster cut into the song, saying, "You

may have heard of him. . . . He goes by the name of Shredderman, and seems to be taking the nation by storm. With Shredderman we have a new breed of superhero. He is, if you will, a *cyber-superhero*—a cutting-edge combination of computer wizardry and vigilantism. With more on this self-proclaimed Champion of Truth and Justice, we turn to correspondent Chatty Adams."

"That's her!" I cried. "That's the pushy lady who was at school today!"

Mom looked at Dad.

Dad looked at Mom.

"Her name's *Chatty?*"

I shrugged and kept watching the TV. What did I care if she had a stupid name? What did she know about Shredderman—that's what I was worried about.

"Thanks, Brian," Chatty said into the camera. "I'm at an elementary school in the quaint town of Cedar Valley, California, where it all began. It seems that Shredderman's quest for truth and justice started when he rescued students here from the classic bad guy—a bully. Apparently he did this by posting the bully's deeds on the World Wide Web, challenging the school's administrators to finally do something about him. Earlier today I asked some students what they thought of Shredderman, and who they suspect this superhero might really be. Here's what they had to say."

They switched to a taped segment, and all of a sudden two of my classmates—Ian McCoy and Randy Ricardo—were on TV. "Yeah," Ian said. "Some kids don't like Shredderman, but those are mostly the ones who got in trouble because of him. The rest of us think Shredderman's totally cool."

"Do you have any idea who he is?" Chatty asked.

"We used to think he was our teacher, Mr. Green—"

"—but it's not," Randy said. "Mr. Green's a hippie."

"*Then* we thought it was our computer lab teacher, Miss Surkit—"

"—but it's not," Randy said. "Miss Surkit's way too short to be a superhero!"

Marvin Speltz's head popped up in between Randy and Ian. "You thought it was Miss *Surkit?* Can you see Miss Surkit posting Bubba's Big Butt on the World Wide Web? She'd get fired! I think it's Mr. Hoover."

"The *janitor?*" Randy and Ian said together.

"Dude. He is *way* into computers," Marvin said.

Chatty Adams was now back live, saying, "As you can see, Brian, there's wide speculation about who is operating behind the Shredderman mask."

"What do the adults think?" the newscaster asked.

"I spoke to a few teachers, but they seem to know about as much as the kids. And the principal"—Chatty looked at her notes—"Dr. Ivana Voss"—she looked back at the camera—"refused to be interviewed." Chatty smiled with only one side of her mouth and said, "I've since found out that Dr. Voss's own *son* went head to head with Shredderman. I don't have to tell you who won."

The newscaster laughed. "No wonder she didn't want to talk to you!"

"Exactly, Brian. And although there are a few people who disagree with Shredderman's tactics, by and large this community seems to think he is one cool dude."

"It sounds like the students have considered that Shredderman might be a woman. . . . What about the possibility that Shredder*man* is really a *boy?*"

"I asked kids that exact question, and here's what they had to say."

My heart started pounding.

My knees felt like jelly.

They ran more of the school tape and Ronnie Stalwess appeared on TV, saying, "No way! Have you seen the site? It's awesome. What kid knows how to do that?" Then Trinity Althoffer said, "A kid? Like a sixth grader or something?" She sniggered. "I don't think so."

They cut from Trinity to a boy I didn't recognize right away.

His hair was sticking out in a couple different directions.

One side of his collar was stuck *inside* his shirt.

The other was flipped up.

He had a streak of peanut butter across one cheek and was stooped a little forward from the weight of his backpack.

Mom grabbed Dad's arm.

Dad held his breath.

My brain felt like it had been dunked in cement.

Did I really look like that?

Chatty Adams held the microphone under her chin and said, "People tell me you're the smartest kid at school. Would *you* know how to put up a site like *shredderman.com?*" Then she stuck the mic right in my face.

"Me?" I said, pointing to myself. "Uh . . . no."

My eyes were shifting around like crazy.

My cheeks were red and twitching.

I'm a terrible liar!

Then I started talking into the microphone really fast, saying, "How could a kid do a site like that? It's got links all over the place. Awesome graphics! It's gotta be done by a professional. Or," I added, "a policeman."

Mom looked at me.

Dad did, too.

And I could tell they were both thinking exactly what Chatty Adams said: "A *policeman?*"

On TV, my eyes were big and bulging, staring right into the camera.

I looked idiotic!

Harebrained!

Really, really stupid!

"Uh-huh," I said, then I spun around and power-walked away from Chatty Adams as fast as I could.

CHAPTER 2
Ambushed

After Dad clicked off the TV, I frowned and asked him, "Why do they even care who Shredderman is? Why can't they just leave it alone?"

"Because people are curious. And they're celebrity hounds."

Shredderman a *celebrity*? Kids said I was the number one nerd at Cedar Valley Elementary. How could *I* be a celebrity?

Mom said to Dad, "I know Nolan registered the site with all the privacy precautions, but don't reporters have ways of getting around that?"

Dad laughed. "Don't worry. *This* reporter tried to get information on who owns *shredderman.com*, but got nowhere."

"Really?" Mom asked.

"Uh-huh. I figured that since Mr. Zilch assigned me to find out who Shredderman is for the *Gazette*, I should at least try it. But what I found out was that unless something illegal is going on or our national security is at risk, they won't tell me who owns the site."

"Did you try bribing them?" Mom asked.

"Try... *bribing* them?"

"Like a reporter who *really* wanted to find out might do?"

"Oh," Dad said, sounding like Mom had squooshed the air out of him.

The phone rang. Dad hurried to get it while Mom called out, "Probably someone who knows how to bribe, wanting to talk to Nolan!"

Dad's head popped back into the room. "Then they'd be calling to talk to you—he used *your* credit card, remember?"

"Oh," Mom said as Dad disappeared around the corner. "That's right."

Two minutes later, Dad was back, saying, "Nolan, that was your sidekick. He's calling a powwow."

"Mr. Green is?" Since when did sidekicks call powwows? That's the superhero's job! "Is he coming over?" I asked.

"No, we're going to his house. He seems to think it would be less conspicuous." Dad shrugged. "He does drive that wild van, and we do live right across the street from the school.... I told him we'd be right over."

A superhero being summoned to his sidekick's lair? Unthinkable! Did sidekicks even *have* lairs? Or caves? Or headquarters? No! They always hung around the superhero's place!

I followed them into the garage. Into the car. "Do you know where he lives?" I asked after I was buckled in.

"He gave me the address," Dad said. "Shouldn't take long."

We drove out of our neighborhood, over the Cedar Creek Bridge, and past the Old Town Square. Then we took a turn off the main road. And another turn onto a gravel road. And another onto a *dirt* road!

It was dark.

Mom was holding on to the dash!

I was bouncing around like crazy!

Maybe my sidekick really *did* live in a cave.

Finally Mom couldn't stand it any longer. "Are we lost, Steven?"

"No, Eve . . . ," Dad said as the car pitched into another pothole. "He did warn me that it would be a bit rough."

"But there's nothing out here! This doesn't even seem like a road anymore! I think we should—"

"There it is!" Dad said, pointing straight ahead.

"Wow," I said as we got closer. "It's a log cabin!"

"That's painted *green*," my mom said, like she'd smelled something stinky.

"Cool!" I said, and it was. The whole place was made out of logs. The walls, the roof, the doors . . . logs, logs, everywhere!

Mr. Green guided us into the living room, saying, "Not conventional, I know, but I dig it."

Mom and Dad were nodding, but they weren't checking things out like I was.

There was a big stone fireplace!

Giant leather furniture!

Old Indian rugs!

And guitars! Guitars everywhere!

"Your house *shreds*, Mr. Green!"

He laughed and said, "Thanks," then asked, "How about some cocoa? I've got it all ready. Just needs to be poured."

"Great!" I said. "Got any marshmallows?"

"I'll put you in charge of marshmallows," he said, then winked at my mom and dad as he led me into the kitchen.

So I put one marshmallow in everyone's mug. Everyone's except mine.

I got three!

Yum-my!

When Mr. Green poured the hot chocolate into the mugs, he said, "So, Nolan. How do you like being in the middle of a media frenzy?"

"Huh? You mean how Chatty Adams is trying to find out who Shredderman is?"

He frowned. "It's not just Chatty Adams, you know."

"Um—well, I wish they'd just leave me alone. But Dad says they can't figure out it's me unless I do something illegal—which, believe me, I won't!"

He nodded and handed me a mug to carry, but he didn't say anything until we were back in the room with Mom and Dad. Then, after everyone had their hot chocolate, he said, "I did not like that Chatty Adams."

"Me neither!" I said. "She was...she was..."

"Meddling? Intrusive?" my dad asked. "Invasive?"

"Yeah!" I said. "It was just like an invasion!"

"Why in the world did the principal allow them on the school grounds?" my mom asked.

Mr. Green said, "Because Ivana Voss would love to find out who Shredderman is."

"Because of how Shredderman trapped her son?" Mom asked.

Mr. Green nodded. "She's still ticked off about that."

I wanted to say something about Dr. Voss's son getting what he deserved, but I didn't. I had the world's softest, tastiest hot-chocolate marshmallow dissolving in my mouth.

Mm-mmmm, good!

But then Mr. Green said, "So what are your plans for the Web site, Nolan?"

"Hmmmm?" I asked through my marshmallow. "Oh. Well, number one: To not do anything illegal."

Mr. Green nodded, but he didn't smile.

And that's when I realized that something was wrong.

My mom noticed, too. She said to him, "Elmo?"

That's right. My sidekick's name is *Elmo.*

Anyway, Mr. Green took a deep breath and said, "Back when Nolan was flying solo on his Web site, I thought he could really use someone to confide in. But now that the two of you are on board…"

I waited, but he didn't really have to finish his sentence. It's funny how missing words can be so much louder than real words. Finally I choked out, "You're saying you don't want to be the Bouncer anymore?"

"It's not that I don't *want* to be, it's just that it's not *necessary* anymore."

"But, Mr. Green!" Suddenly I didn't want cocoa. Or marshmallows. What was he *doing*? Sidekicks don't quit!

Sidekicks *can't* quit!

"I understand, Elmo," my dad was saying. "You're in a touchy position at the school. Especially since Dr. Voss is no fan of Shredderman."

Mr. Green nodded. "I wouldn't do this if Nolan didn't have the two of you. But he does, and really, it's just a matter of time."

"Before what?" I demanded.

The three of them looked at me. Finally Mr. Green said, "Before they unmask you, Nolan."

"No way!" I cried. "They're not going to do it! I won't let them!"

One by one, the three of them looked down.

"Mom?" I asked. "Dad . . . ?"

Finally my dad said, "I do think it might be a good idea to cool it for a while, champ."

"But—"

"Plus," my mom said, "have you thought about the trouble your dad will be in if people do find out?"

"What do you mean?" I couldn't believe this. They were all ganging up on me!

This was a total ambush!

"What I mean is, your father's been telling Mr. Zilch that he's getting to the bottom of who Shredderman is. What do you think Mr. Zilch will do when he finds out that your father's known all along who Shredderman is?"

"You don't think . . . you don't think they'd *fire* him, do you?" I turned to my dad. "He can't *fire* you, can he?"

Dad shrugged. "He won't take kindly to it, I can tell you that."

Everyone was quiet for a minute, until my mom said, "Why don't you lie low for a while, Nolan? Just until things cool off."

Until they cooled off? When would *that* be?

My lips felt all sticky.

My throat felt choked.

And in my stomach, the world's fluffiest marshmallow felt like a rock.

I knew what they were really saying.

It was time for Shredderman to stop.

CHAPTER 3
Into the Fire

I went to bed mad.

What kind of superhero has his sidekick quit on him?

What kind of superhero has parents who tell him what to do?

Sheez.

But there was no arguing with my parents.

So what if I'm a superhero?

They're *adults*.

When I woke up at 5:37 a.m., I was still mad. So I got out of bed.

I booted up my computer.

I went to *shredderman.com*. It had been a long time since I'd played around on my own site. It was a great site! A fun site. Lots of cool links. Lots of cool graphics. Lots of funny jokes.

I'd worked so hard on it!

No way was I going to tear this down!

No way was I going to stop fighting for truth and justice!

I was going to make my site bigger and better than ever!

"Honey?" Mom tapped on my door and opened it. "I saw the light on."

"I'm busy," I grumbled.

"Oh, dear," she said, and came in anyway. And when she saw that I was working on my site, she frowned. "I thought we decided you'd lie low for a while."

"*You* decided," I said.

"But, honey..."

22

Sheez. I'd never get anything done with her looking over my shoulder. So instead of arguing, I shut down my computer and headed for the bathroom.

"Honey...?" she said again, following along.

"Do you mind, Mom?" I asked, closing the bathroom door in her face. "I need some privacy."

I could hear Mom and Dad talking about me in the hallway.

I couldn't tell what they were saying, but I knew they were not happy.

Well, fine.

Let them be mad.

It had all been some cute, childish game to them.

Well, truth and justice were *not* cute. They were *not* a game!

They were...They were...*everything*.

I looked at myself in the mirror.

Man, my hair was a mess! It was sticking out everywhere!

I tried wetting it down, but *boiiiiing*, it shot back out.

I filled up the sink and dunked my head in.

Brrrrrr!

And now I was stuck. I couldn't reach the towel!

So I dripped across the bathroom, rubbed my hair with the towel, then went back to the mirror.

I looked wild!

Crazy!

Hmmmm. Maybe I should just leave my hair like that.

I took out some gel and went to town, rubbing it all through my hair. I spiked it up.

Looked kinda cool.

I combed it straight back.

I looked like an evil warlord.

I spiked it back up.

I kinda liked it.

I combed it regular.

Bor-ing.

I spiked it back up. . . .

Mom knocked. "Nolan?"

"What!"

"You've just been in there a long time. Are you all right?"

What was she thinking? That I'd flushed myself? Why couldn't they just leave me alone?

"Nolan?"

That did it. I took one last look at myself.

I was going to school spiked. Mom practically fainted when I opened the door.

I stepped past her.

"Son?" Dad asked when he saw me.

"Don't touch it," I growled, then went to my room to get dressed for school.

CHAPTER 4
Escape

At school, Mr. Green acted like everything was normal.

He was cheerful.

Friendly.

He strummed his guitar between lessons and reminded us that, "Attitude is everything!"

For the first time ever, I wanted to call him the Happy Hippie, just like Bubba Bixby always had.

Then, during social studies, Trinity leaned over and whispered, "I like your hair."

I almost told her to shut up and quit making fun of me, but she was smiling.

Nicely.

So really I didn't know *what* to say.

Then she whispered, "Everyone's saying it looks great."

"They are?"

"Uh-huh."

Randy and Freddy at our table overheard, because they snickered and said, "Yeah, whatcha trying to be? A babe magnet?"

"Shut up, stupid," Trinity told them. "Like you even know what style is."

They all pulled faces at each other.

No one else said anything about my hair, though. And at lunch I sat by myself again.

Some babe magnet.

When school let out, I was in a worse mood than ever. Mr. Green called my name as I was leaving, but I just power-walked out of there. What did I care what he wanted to say?

The quitter.

I kept right on power-walking, too. Across the

blacktop, through the teachers' parking lot, across the street, straight for home.

Only I didn't want to be *there*, either.

It was strange. I hate being alone. I hate having no friends. But the minute I crossed the street, I *wanted* to be alone.

At least I didn't want to have to talk to my mom.

Or even hide in my room. Being around my computer would just remind me that I couldn't do the one thing that made me feel like I *wasn't* alone. The one thing that made me feel like I *did* have friends.

Being Shredderman had helped me through the whole school year. It had helped me tame the world's biggest bully—Bubba Bixby. It had helped me learn that being the school nerd didn't mean that people didn't like you.

It meant they didn't *know* you.

Yet.

How could the three people who *did* know me—my mom and dad and Mr. Green—expect me to give up the one thing that made me feel good?

And that's why I didn't even open the front door of my house. Instead, I snuck into the garage, grabbed my bike, put on my helmet, and headed out.

I didn't know where I was going. I didn't know how long I'd be gone. I just knew I wanted to be away from school and home.

I pedaled with all my might. Up hills. Down hills. I flew over the Cedar Creek Bridge. Past Old Town! Past the *Gazette* building! Past the police station! The fire station! I turned off the main road and zoomed down streets I didn't even know existed, pedaling until my lungs hurt.

Finally I pulled to the side of the road.

My legs were shaky.

My head was pouring sweat.

My backpack felt like it weighed a ton. Why hadn't I left it at home?

I looked around.

Where *was* I?

I made a U-turn and started coasting back the way I'd come. But after a while, I started wondering if I was going the right way. Had I missed a turn? If I was on the right road, why didn't anything look familiar?

I rode a while longer, then stopped again and looked around.

I was lost!

A bubble of panic was rising inside me. Plus, I was dying of thirst. And still so sweaty! Maybe I should have told Mom where I was going. She would have made me pack a juice box.

Okay, I told myself. Try to calm down. All you have to do is get back to Old Town. There's a water fountain at Old Town, and getting home from there is easy. Ask someone how to get to Old Town!

So I pushed on and flagged down the first car that came along. "Hey!" I shouted, waving my arm like crazy. "Can you tell me how to get to Old Town?"

"Sure!" the man shouted back. "Keep going the way you're going, then take a right, a left, and another right. Just like that—turn, turn, turn," he said, zigzagging his hand. "It'll take you right there!"

"Thanks!" I called, and he zoomed off.

So I pedaled like mad until I came to the first cross street.

I turned right!

I pedaled like mad until I came to the next cross street.

I turned left!

I pedaled like double-mad until I came to the next cross street.

I turned right!

Can I follow directions, or what?

Then I rode along, keeping my eyes peeled. It didn't *look* like uphill...why was it so hard to pedal?

And it sure didn't seem like I was near Old Town. Where *was* I?

I got off my bike and looked around.

No houses.

No cars.

No people.

Just trees, everywhere I looked.

And when I saw my back tire, my stomach did a loop-de-loop.

I was in the middle of nowhere.

With a flat!

CHAPTER 5
Where the River Meets the Road

Uh-triple-oh! I was going to be in trou-uh-ble when I got home. *If* I could figure out where home was!

I checked my bike tire.

It was definitely flat.

I tried riding it a little anyway.

It was worse than walking.

So I got off and pushed my bike along the road, looking for houses. There had to be a house here somewhere! Why else was there a road?

When I got tired of pushing, I just stood on the shoulder of the road for a while, waiting for someone to come by. That's all I had to do, I told myself—wait. I'd flag someone down. I'd have them call my mom and explain where I was. She'd come pick me up!

But I waited a long time, and no one came by. So finally I hid my bike behind some trees and started walking. I didn't want to leave my back-pack, because it was full of all the things that matter most to me. Like my digital camera.

My collapsible periscope!

Binoculars!

You know, stuff any cyber-superhero carries around with him.

Not that being a cyber-superhero was doing me a bit of good, being lost in the woods. But still, spy tools are expensive! I sure didn't want them to be stolen. Or carried off by squirrels!

So I lugged them along and just kept walking.

And walking.

And walking!

And I tried to walk fast, but I was tired. And thirsty!

Man, was I thirsty!

I was also—*shhhhhh*—scared.

I kept telling myself that if I just stayed on the road, I was bound to run into *something*.

Some*one*.

But the farther I walked, the more trees there seemed to be. This road was leading me to the *middle* of the middle of nowhere!

And even though it wasn't dark yet, I could tell the sun was on its way down. The road was getting really, really shady.

I got to the top of a little hill, and down on the other side there was a wide wooden bridge. No cars. No people. But the bridge made me feel better. It wasn't nearly as big as the Cedar Creek Bridge, but it proved that this wasn't just a road to nowhere. It went to a bridge that took you across a river and...

A river!

I ran down the road as fast as I could.

Water!

I crunched through the leaves and pine needles, down the riverbank to the stream. Wa-hoo! Water!

I found a steady rock, out a ways where the water was flowing strong and clean.

Didn't want to get sick from stagnant water!

I cupped my hands and drank.

And drank!

And drank!

It was delicious!

The best-tasting water ever!

And when I'd finally had enough to drink, I backed off the rock and started up the riverbank.

I felt *tons* better.

Like I could walk to the moon!

Maybe even to Mars!

Of course, that's 100 million kilometers away, and there isn't any water on Mars—except for *maybe* some at the poles—so that was probably exaggerating a little.

But I *could* find my way home.

Piece of cake!

I climbed up the bank and was just getting past the boulders to the trees when a car came thumping over the bridge. I yelled "Wait!" and tried to run out to the road, but I slipped on a bed of pine needles and fell instead.

Some superhero, huh?

I knew it was too late. I knew there was no way he saw me. And I was busy thinking, Drat! when the strangest thing happened.

The car pulled off the road and stopped.

I almost ran out to it, but I didn't. For some reason the car looked ... *sinister*.

It was long.

Sleek.

Black.

And it was just sitting there, giving me the creeps.

I crouched behind a tree, and now I was worried that the driver *had* seen me.

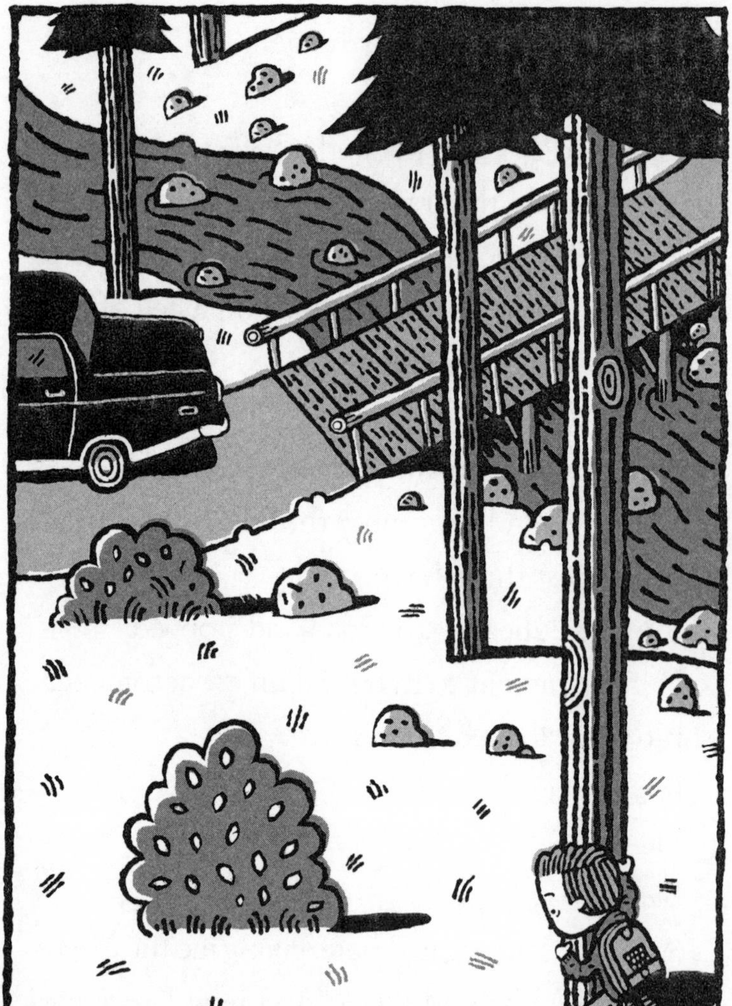

I waited for him to do something, but he didn't. He just sat there in his sinister black car for the longest time.

I crouched lower. Was he waiting for me to come out? Was he planning to . . . *kidnap* me?

Very slowly I took out my digital camera.

I took out my binoculars.

If I was going to get kidnapped, maybe I could leave some evidence behind. Evidence that would help my mom and dad get me back!

I looked at the car through my binoculars. I could see a man sitting in the driver's seat. He seemed to be looking in his rearview mirror.

What was he doing?

What was he waiting for?

Then the door opened and he got out.

He was wearing a black hat.

Black gloves!

Shiny black shoes and a gray *trench* coat.

I crouched lower. This guy hadn't stopped for

me. He had no idea I was there! So what was he doing there, wearing a hat and gloves and a trench coat?

In the *woods*.

I put my digital camera lens up to one of my binoculars' eyepieces. I held the camera and binoculars together tight, then zoomed in on the guy, and *click*. I took a picture of him.

I checked the image in the display monitor of my camera.

Nice and sharp!

I watched the trench coat guy look around. Over one shoulder. Over the other. Then he reached back inside the car and took out a...What *was* that? A *boulder*?

Yes! The guy had a *boulder*.

What was he up to?

I took another picture of him with the boulder.

Another nice shot!

The man looked over both shoulders again, then started walking my way.

Across the road.

Into the woods.

Closer.

And closer!

CHAPTER 6
X Marks the Spot!

Something strange was going on. Why in the world would a guy in a trench coat and shiny shoes stomp through the woods with a boulder?

I scrunched down lower.

And lower.

And just when I thought for sure he was going to see me, he took one last look over his shoulder then turned, slip-sliding on pine needles as he went down to the river.

He hurried over to the bridge.

He went under the bridge!

I watched him through my binoculars, scooting over a few trees so I could keep an eye on him.

I lost him in the shadows of the bridge for a minute.

Two minutes.

Not knowing where he was made me nervous. Had he figured out I was there? Could he be sneaking up behind me?

Did he have a gun?

Then I spotted him coming out from under the bridge. Looking left. Looking right. Hiking back up the riverbank.

Only now both his arms were swinging free.

No boulder.

I watched him get back into his car, and right before he drove away I zoomed in and took a picture of the car.

When he was gone, I just stayed put a minute,

thinking. Obviously this guy was doing something sneaky. Maybe even illegal.

But with a *boulder*?

The car was long gone by the time I decided to investigate. I strapped on my backpack, then hurried down to the bridge. And believe me, I was on the serious lookout for anyone around.

I also wanted to hurry because it was cooling off quick, and the shadows were very long.

The sun was going down!

Or, really, the earth was rotating away from the sun, making it *look* like the sun was going down.

Anyway, I hurried under the bridge and checked all around.

Boulders, boulders, everywhere!

I found one about the size of the trench coat guy's and went to pick it up.

It weighed a ton!

Well, okay, it wasn't really two thousand pounds. It was more like fifty or sixty pounds. But still! How had the trench coat guy carried something that heavy under one arm? Was he Hercules in disguise?

Wait a minute—maybe it wasn't a real boulder. Maybe it was like one of those fake rocks they use in the movies.

But why would he bring a fake rock down to the river?

I picked up a stick and started poking at boulders. Any boulder that was about the right size, I jabbed.

Clonk. Clonk. Clonk. They were all solid. Didn't budge an inch.

Then, about halfway under the bridge, I jabbed at a boulder and it went *thump*.

I jabbed again.

Thump.

It sure looked like a boulder. It even had moss growing on it!

I looked left.

I looked right.

The water running downstream made it hard to hear anything else. If someone came along, I'd never hear them.

I reached for the boulder, and that's when I noticed that the moss was *glued* on.

In the shape of an X!

My heart started pounding.

My skin started creeping.

X marks the spot!

I picked up the boulder.

Compared to a real boulder, it weighed hardly anything!

I turned it over. There was a secret door!

I twisted the latch and opened the door.

And when I saw what was inside, I knew I had to get out of there.

Quick!

CHAPTER 7
Things Turn Shabby

I'd never seen so much money in my life. I pulled out a stack that was rubber-banded together and fanned through it.

Wow.

They were all Benjamin Franklins.

All one-hundred-dollar bills!

And maybe Benjamin Franklin was never a United States president, but he definitely deserves to be on the one-hundred-dollar bill.

He invented the fire engine.

The post office.

The library.

He discovered electricity!

How many presidents can say *that*?

And, I asked myself, how much time was I going to waste thinking about Benjamin Franklin while I was in danger under a bridge?

I looked around quick, then pulled out more stacks and fanned through them, trying to do a speedy count of the money in the boulder. Ten stacks, a hundred bills each, a hundred dollars each...

Holy hollow boulder, Batman! There was a hundred thousand dollars in this rock!

Talk about electricity—boy, was I charged!

Then all of a sudden, the bridge *thump-thump-thumped* overhead.

Uh-triple-oh!

What if the trench coat guy was back?

I stuffed all the money into the rock, put the rock back where I'd found it, then scrambled up the riverbank, staying under the bridge.

I really wanted to get *out* of there, but I couldn't risk being seen.

I had to hide!

I found a place way up the bank, behind a pillar of cement that was helping to hold up the bridge.

I held my breath.

One minute.

Two!

Finally I let it out and tried to think. What if no one was up there? I couldn't *hear* anyone up there. What if I was hiding from no one? How long was I going to sit there, hiding from no one?

Very quietly, I took my periscope out of my backpack.

I extended it up, up, up, until it was peeking over the planks of the bridge.

I turned it left.

I turned it right.

There *was* a car up there!

It wasn't sleek and black, though. It was small. And tan. And sort of banged up.

The man coming out of it didn't give me the creeps like the trench coat guy had, either. He was just a regular-looking guy. But he *was* acting kind of nervous.

I put my digital camera up to the periscope's eyepiece.

He looked over one shoulder.

I clicked.

He looked over the other shoulder.

I clicked again.

He started coming across the bridge.

I collapsed my periscope fast and put it away.

And then I saw him with my own naked eyes, stumbling down the riverbank. His hair was messy and his clothes were kind of shabby. He was actually the opposite of the trench coat guy. He looked really...unkempt.

Slovenly.

Bedraggled!

Did he know about the money?

Nah, he probably just had to do an emergency pee. No way a shabby guy like him knew someone as slick as the trench coat guy.

I watched him, thinking that maybe when he was done with his emergency, I'd ask him how to get back to Old Town. Maybe I could even get him to call my mom.

I stayed hidden, though. I didn't want to embarrass him! But he didn't stop at a tree or anything. And I started thinking, Hey, guy— don't get so close to the river! People *drink* out of that, you know! But he kept on going straight down to the water. Then he turned and came under the bridge.

He was looking for the rock!

He was about to become $100,000 richer.

But *why?*

He went from boulder to boulder until he saw it: X marks the spot.

He looked around.

I ducked behind the pillar!

He picked up the rock.

I zoomed in on him with my camera!

He opened the bottom of the boulder.

I clicked!

He looked around.

I clicked again!

Boy, was he nervous.

Boy, was I nervous, too!

Then he unzipped his jacket and wrestled something out of the back of his pants.

He'd been hiding a stack of papers back there!

He put the papers on the ground and started cramming bundles of money down his pants. Pretty soon the boulder was empty and the guy had the hundred thousand dollars stashed.

In his underwear!

He folded the papers and crammed them into the rock. He closed the secret door. He was looking around like crazy, shaking like mad!

When he was done, he put the boulder back and raced out of there so fast that he fell twice on his hundred-thousand-dollar butt before making it up the riverbank.

Wow.

What had the shabby guy put into the boulder?

What in the world was worth one hundred thousand dollars to the trench coat man?

The minute I heard the car drive off, I raced down to the boulder.

I opened it.

I pulled out the papers.

I unfolded them and saw...diagrams and numbers. Pages and pages of calculations!

Equations!

Formulas!

And at the top of every page, stamped in red, was "CLASSIFIED."

It didn't take a rocket scientist—or even a superhero—to figure out that something was fishy. Stinky, smelly, fishy! And what's amazing is that I'd had the chance to take the money, but I hadn't. That would have felt like stealing.

But taking these calculations—whatever they were—didn't feel like stealing. It felt like I was *saving* them. "CLASSIFIED" meant they were important. Top-secret! No way the shabby guy should be selling them!

I crammed the papers into my backpack. I returned the boulder to where I'd found it.

I couldn't go back to the road now. What if the trench coat guy or the shabby guy came back? What if they saw me? Walking along the road was too dangerous!

Instead, I headed upstream, into the darkening forest.

CHAPTER 8
Lost and Found

Walking away from the road and into the forest wasn't as dumb as it sounds. I was walking *up*stream, and I knew that Cedar Creek ran *down* through town. Eventually I'd have to come to the Cedar Creek Bridge, and from there I'd know how to get home.

I was hurrying, too! I didn't want anyone to see me near the little bridge where I'd found the fake boulder.

At first I was only worried about the trench coat guy catching me. But after I'd walked a long way, I started worrying more about spending the night in the forest. It was getting dark fast!

So I ran the best I could. Through sand and

mud and rocks, I kept moving upstream, hoping the Cedar Creek Bridge would pop into view.

It didn't. And I was just starting to really panic when I saw something through the pine trees.

I wasn't dying of thirst or falling down dead in the desert or anything, but... was that a *mirage*?

No!

It really was a log cabin!

A *green* log cabin!

I ran toward it like crazy, and when I got close

enough, I started shouting, "Mr. Green! Mr. Green!"

He came out through the front door, looking around, and when he saw me, he said, "Nolan?"

"Mr. Green!" I cried.

"Are you all right?"

"I was lost! I was riding my bike but it got a flat, so I started walking, but then this..." And then I remembered—Mr. Green wasn't the Bouncer anymore. He'd quit! I couldn't tell him about the trench coat guy or the shabby guy—he'd tell me to lie low!

So I took a deep breath and said, "I got lost, that's all."

He looked at his watch. "Your parents must be worried."

I nodded.

I followed him inside, where he let me call my mom. And when she heard it was me, the first thing she said was, "Oh, honey! Oh, honey, you're okay!" Then she called over to my dad, "Steven! It's him! He's fine!" Then, like a light switch, she clicked on the anger. "Nolan, *why* did you leave without saying where you were going? What were you thinking? Do you know how worried we've been? Just because things are not going exactly the way you want them to doesn't mean you can thumb your nose at us and start throwing around attitude!"

And that was just her warm-up! She was getting *really* worked up when Mr. Green took the phone away from me and told her he'd be happy to drive me home.

After he hung up, he smiled at me and said, "Don't sweat it too much, Nolan. That's just how parents get when they've been worried."

I followed him to his van without a word. I was back to feeling sick inside. I wanted to tell Mr. Green and my parents about the trench coat guy and the shabby guy, but I couldn't. It would get me in more trouble than I already was. And boy, was I in *major* trouble with Mom and Dad.

But still, I had to do something!

And I had to do it without the trench coat guy or the shabby guy finding out who I was.

There was only one answer—Shredderman.

So after Mr. Green dropped me off and Mom and Dad were done scolding me, I ate cold chicken and beans and went straight to bed.

Only I didn't go straight to sleep!

I lay in bed, waiting.

And thinking.

And when the house was finally quiet and I was sure my parents were asleep, I got up, booted up, and went to work. First I scanned in all the pages of calculations and diagrams that I'd pulled out of the fake boulder.

Always smart to make a backup!

Then I got to work putting together a Photoshop page. I moved a picture of the trench coat guy next to a picture of the shabby guy, and added a shot of the "CLASSIFIED" pages. Then between the images I wrote:

Why
would this
guy . . .

Pay this guy . . .

$100,000!

*For a dozen
pages of these?*

CLASSIFIED

*I think you should investigate! (And check your snail
mail. I'm sending you the classified documents.)*

Yours in Truth and Justice,

Shredderman

Then I sneaked down the hall and booted up
my mom's computer.

I went to her e-mail.

I checked her address book.

I found him!

Sergeant William Klubb—my dad's friend at the police station. And his e-mail was easy: wklubb@cvpd.gov.net.

Oh, yeah!

I tiptoed back to my bedroom, attached the Photoshop file to an e-mail, and sent it to Sarge with "URGENT" in the message box. Then I tagged it with a red exclamation mark and sent it into cyberspace.

Step one, complete!

Step two, mail the documents.

I looked up the address of the Cedar Valley Police Department on the Internet, then printed out a mailing label addressed to Sergeant William Klubb.

I typed up a return label: Sergeant William Klubb, same address! Whether it went forward or backward, it would get to him.

Then I shut down my computer and started stuffing the envelope.

Documents in!

Labels on!

Sealed with tape (saliva has DNA)!

Then I slapped a bunch of stamps on the envelope and wrestled my feet into my shoes. And I was starting to climb out my window to go mail it, but at the last minute I turned around and scrawled a note that said:

Don't be mad! I'll be right back!

Nolan

(2:10 a.m.)

Then I climbed out my window.

I landed *whoosh*, like a cat. I zoomed up the street. Around the corner.

There it was—the neighborhood mailbox.

I slid the envelope down the hatch.

I whispered "Good luck!" and zoomed back home.

By 2:16 a.m., I was back inside. Am I speedy, or what? I fell into bed happy. Happy to be Shredderman.

CHAPTER 9
Busted

In the morning, Mom was real nice when she woke me up. "Nolan..." She was stroking my hair. "Nolan, honey, it's time to get up."

For a minute I forgot that I was mad at her. And that she'd been mad at me. The way she was stroking my hair felt so nice.

Then my dad came in, saying, "Hey, champ. I think I figured out what road you left your bike on." He had a map, and squashed my leg when he squeezed onto my bed to show me.

"Ow!" I said, and rolled toward the wall. Boy, did I sound grumpy!

Mom stood up and said, "Come on, Nolan. You

can do better than that. Help your father find your bike while I make us all some breakfast."

So I sat up and looked at the map. "Where?"

"Well, here's where Mr. Green lives," Dad said, pointing. "And if you follow the river this way, the first road you come across is this one—Blackstone Way."

I studied the map, trying to figure out where I'd gone and where I'd gone wrong. But then Dad said, "If you'd stuck to the road, you'd have been home free, Nolan." He pointed. "A quarter mile, max, and you'd have been on Leeward, then *vroom*, straight out to Old Town." He shook his head. "I still don't understand why you left the road. Do you have any idea how dangerous that was? How could we have ever found you? What were you *thinking*?"

I shrugged and looked away. It did seem really, really stupid, but that's because I couldn't tell him the truth.

"Well," Dad sighed. Then he stood up and said, "I'll go out there and see if I can find your bike."

"Can I go with you?"

He looked at his watch. "You won't have time before school."

"So? I'll just—"

"No. You will go to school like you're supposed to." He said it real sternly, then took a deep breath and said, "If I can't find it on my own, I'll take you back out there after school."

"But—"

"No ifs, ands, or buts, Nolan. Just tell me which side of the road, and how far from the bridge you think it is."

I could tell I wasn't going to get him to change his mind, so I started calculating out loud. "If you're walking toward the bridge, it's on the right side of the road. And I walked for...forty-five minutes?"

"How fast?"

"As fast as I could." I thought for a minute. The fastest I'd run a mile at school was nine minutes. Call it ten. If I was going even half that speed, I'd be going one mile in twenty minutes.

That made three miles in sixty minutes.

Three miles an hour?

Sheez. Some kind of superhero.

Finally I said, "It's probably about two miles from the bridge."

"Good enough," Dad said, folding the map. "I'll do my best." He slapped my leg. "Now hustle up!"

"Uh...," I said when he'd reached the door, "thanks, Dad."

He turned to face me. "Thank me by not pulling a stunt like that again."

"It wasn't a stunt, Dad!"

"Well, whatever you call it, don't do anything like it again."

I looked down. "I'm sorry."

"We'll talk more when I get home tonight,

okay? I know you're mad about Shredderman, and I do understand that. For now, try to see more than just your side of it, okay? We'll figure some way to work this out."

I nodded, but I didn't believe him. "Working it out" meant lying low. Boy! If they knew what was going on, I'd be in some boiling hot water!

I did lie low at school, though. Even lower than usual. I didn't even play four-square or go to the computer lab at recess. I just went down to the swings and sat on the edge of the sand, looking at birds peck around the lower field.

Then out of nowhere, my dad showed up in the cafeteria at lunch. He sat right across the table from me. It was strange to have him suddenly appear in the cafeteria, but I could tell something big was on his mind.

"You couldn't find my bike?" I asked him.

"Oh, I found your bike, all right," he said. "It took me nearly two hours, but I found it. And I got the flat fixed, too. It's back in the garage, good as new."

"Wow, Dad. Thanks!" I really was happy. From the way he was acting, I thought for sure he was going to say my bike was ruined. But it was fine. Fixed! Ready to ride!

So why was he frowning?

"Dad?" I asked him. "What's wrong?"

He was looking around. "Why are you here all by yourself?"

"Huh? Oh." I shrugged. "This is where I eat."

"Every day?"

I nodded.

"Always by yourself?"

I shrugged and nodded some more.

"Why aren't you eating with...with some friends?"

"Dad, *shhhh*. It's okay. I'm used to it."

"But—" He was shaking his head. "Nolan, I had no idea..."

He was making me feel worse than I already did about having no friends. So I switched the subject. "Thanks for coming here to tell me about my bike, Dad."

He focused on me and said, "I didn't actually come here because of that. I came here because...because Sergeant Klubb called me."

Uh-oh.

I tried to act cool. "Oh, yeah?"

"Apparently he got an e-mail from Shredderman. Sarge wanted to know if I'd made any progress figuring out who he is."

Brother. It'd only been half a day. Couldn't anyone give a superhero a break?

"Nolan?"

"What, Dad?"

"You're not denying it? I thought for sure it was some other guy pretending to be you."

I shrugged.

"It *was* you?"

His lips got tight.

His eyes got twitchy.

Finally he whispered, "What do you think you're *doing?*"

My lips got tight right back.

I made my eyes into little slits.

I leaned forward and whispered, "Fighting for truth and justice, like I'm supposed to!"

We stared each other down for a solid minute. Then he stood and said, "You're coming home."

"But—"

"You're coming home!"

He grabbed me by the arm and dragged me out of there. I had my backpack, but he wouldn't even let me get my homework books! He marched me across school, stuck his head in the office door, and called out to Mrs. Holler, "I'm taking Nolan home!"

"Uh...," she said, then leaned out the office door, calling, "Wait a minute, Mr. Byrd! Is this for illness, or what?"

"It's for attitude!" he shouted back at her. Then he hustled me across the street.

CHAPTER 10
Diabolical Deeds

"All right," Dad said when he'd muscled me through our front door. "Show me what you e-mailed to Sarge."

I thought about saying no. If he didn't want to help fight for truth and justice, then why should he get to know what I was doing? But I'd never seen my dad this upset before, and I was feeling bad and a little scared. Not of him, but of him not liking me anymore. Maybe I didn't have any friends at school, but at home I had two really good ones.

Or at least I used to.

So I led him down to my room.

There were messages in my Shredderman in-box—one was from wklubb@cvpd.gov.net. I was dying to know what Sarge had mailed me, but I clicked on the SENT folder and opened the e-mail I'd sent Sarge instead. "Here," I said, and let my dad sit down.

He looked at the pictures and read the words slowly. Out loud. "Why would this guy... Pay this guy... A hundred thousand dollars... For a dozen pages of these? I think you should investigate. And check your snail mail. I'm sending you the classified documents." He turned to me and asked, "Nolan, who *are* these people you took pictures of? When did you... Where did you... *How* did you...?" He couldn't seem to finish his sentences. But then he practically spit out, "*What* classified documents?"

"The ones I snail-mailed to Sarge."

"The ones you..."

He took me by the shoulders.

He looked me square in the eye.

"Nolan, start from the beginning, and tell me everything."

He wasn't looking angry.

Or even upset.

He looked worried.

"It's okay, Dad. They didn't see me! I was getting a drink from the river because I was so, so, *so* thirsty. I'd been lost for hours! I'd been walking, and my backpack was heavy, and I knew Mom would be mad at me, and—"

"Nolan! The men. Where did you see these men?"

"At a bridge on the road where I hid my bike. The guy with the trench coat stopped first. I was going to ask him to call you, but he took that boulder out of his car and..."

"Boulder? What boulder?"

I took my digital camera out of my backpack, connected it to my computer, and started a slide show for my dad, showing him all the pictures I'd taken of the trench coat guy and the shabby guy, explaining what had happened as I went along.

When I was done, Dad said, "This is incredible. It sounds like something out of a cartoon. Or a Cold War spy mission or something!"

"Cold War? What's that?"

He looked at me, then took a deep breath and nodded. "It was more a situation than a war. The United States and the Soviet Union tried to learn each other's secrets. There was a lot of spying going on. And among the spies were traitors—people selling their own country's secrets for cash or diamonds or whatever."

"Wow." I looked back at the computer monitor. "Do you think these guys are *spies?*"

"Like I said, it seems incredible. But that boulder is sure clandestine."

"Clandestine?"

"You know—sneaky. Cloak-and-dagger. Underhanded."

"Oh."

"Someone would notice a briefcase by a river,

but the boulder could sit there for days. Weeks!"

"So do you think they're spies, Dad? Or traitors?"

My dad frowned and tapped the trench coat guy on my monitor. "Well, this turkey is sure *dressed* like a spy." He looked at me and said, "Nolan, why didn't you just tell your mother and me about this?"

I shrugged. "Because you don't want me to be Shredderman anymore!"

"We never said that!"

"But that *is* what you want."

"No, it's not! We just want you to..." He took a deep breath, trying to calm down. "Look, Nolan. Shredderman aside, if you had told your mother and me about this, we could have taken all the information directly to the police. There was no reason to hide behind the Shredderman mask!"

I just stared at him. Going to the police as Nolan Byrd had never even crossed my mind.

He shook his head.

He scratched an ear.

He sighed, and sighed again.

"Okay," he finally said, "I want to catch Mom up on what's going on. Maybe Mr. Green, too." He shook his head again. "Talk about being in the wrong place at the wrong time! If this is as serious as it seems, do you realize what these men might have done to you if they'd seen you?"

I shrugged. "But they didn't see me."

He dropped his voice and held my shoulders. "But they know someone saw *them*."

"What do you mean?"

He hitched a thumb at my monitor. "Mr. Trench Coat there didn't get what he paid for."

"But he doesn't know *I* took the papers."

Dad nodded. It was a real serious nod. Then he took a deep breath and headed for the phone, saying, "We've got to make sure it stays that way."

CHAPTER 11
Uh-Triple-Oh!

Mom always gets home from her job as a computer programmer before I get home from school at 3:05. She even works from home some days—like when I'm sick, or have some school event she wants to go to. Mom says working at Tech-Key lets her have the best of both worlds. Dad says he wishes Mr. Zilch was even half as understanding about his hours at the *Gazette*.

But there it was, 2:30 in the afternoon, and we were all three someplace we weren't supposed to be—home.

We'd gone over everything three times.

Maybe four!

But Mom was still pacing around. Shaking her

head. Throwing her hands in the air. All she could seem to say was, "But, Steven, what are we going to *do* about it?"

Then the phone rang.

Mom looked at Dad.

Dad looked at Mom.

They agreed to let the answering machine pick up, and we all waited through "You've reached Eve 'n' Steven's. Please leave a message at the beep."

A gruff voice said, "Steven, if you're there, pick up!"

Dad pulled a face at Mom that said *Uh-oh*, but Mom held his arm and whispered, "He doesn't know you're here."

"Steven!" the voice barked. "Look, man, I'm getting heat from all angles. I need everything you've got on Shredderman, and I need it now!"

Uh-triple-oh!

It seemed like the caller was starting to hang

up, but then his voice was back, snapping, "And why don't you have your cell phone on?"

Click.

"Ho-boy," Dad sighed.

"Was that Mr. Zilch?" I whispered.

"Yes, it was." He kissed my mom on the forehead. "Guess I'd better get to the *Gazette*, pronto."

"What are you going to tell him?" my mom asked.

Dad looked at her and shook his head. "I have no idea." Then he looked at me. "But I'm afraid it can't be the truth."

The minute they were out of the room, I zoomed over to my computer and clicked on my in-box.

I opened the e-mail Sarge had sent me.

It was short.

To the point.

Shredderman: Please call the CVPD. We need to talk ASAP.

Talk to him? I couldn't do that! There was no way I could disguise my voice enough! What was I going to do?

I was lost in thought, running through some crazy ideas, when Mom called, "Nolan! Nolan, come quick!"

I ran into the living room where she was looking out the window, her hand held up to her mouth.

"What, Mom?"

She just pointed across the street to the school.

My jaw dropped.

My eyes popped.

Police cars were blocking the teachers' parking lot! Their blue lights were flashing like crazy! I tore down to my room and got my backpack. I pulled out my binoculars and looked at the parking lot. There were kids all over the place!

And teachers!

And...Oh, no! There was Chatty Adams and her camera crew!

Then I spotted Sergeant Klubb putting someone in the backseat of his police car!

My heart sank.

They were arresting Mr. Green!

CHAPTER 12
No Time for TV

"Why are they arresting Mr. Green?" I cried.

"Calm down, Nolan," my mom said. "We don't know that he's being arrested. Maybe they just... maybe they just want to ask him some questions."

"Like *what*?"

She shook her head but didn't answer. Instead, she said, "I'd better call your father."

I stayed glued to the window. Chatty Adams was chasing after Sarge, sticking her microphone in his face. She even tried to block his way into the police car!

Finally Sarge managed to get past her. He dove into the car and drove away.

I left the window and ran to Mom's desk, where she was punching buttons on the phone. "He's not answering at work yet," she muttered. "I sure hope he turned on his cell phone." She finished dialing and waited while it rang. "Steven? Oh, thank heavens. They just took Elmo off in a police car...Uh-huh...Uh-huh...No, no hand-cuffs...I don't know!" She listened for a minute, then said, "Well, call us the minute you find something out, okay?"

I ran down to my room.

Mom ran after me. "Nolan! What are you doing?"

I was sitting at my computer, typing like mad.

"Nolan, stop!"

"Mom, I have to help Mr. Green!"

"Stop!" She read the message I was writing Sarge:

Elmo Green is not Shredderman!

Let him go.

She knelt beside me and said, "Nolan, honey, stop. Stop and take a deep breath. You've got to stop shooting from the hip. Take the time to think this through."

"But they arrested Mr. Green! They think he's Shredderman!"

"Has Shredderman done anything that would get him arrested?"

"No!" I stared at her. "At least I don't think so..."

"So you see? That almost certainly is *not* what's happening to Mr. Green."

"But—"

"Let's wait and see, okay? And when we find out more, we'll go from there."

Just then the phone rang. Mom stood up and raced to get it, saying, "That's probably your dad now."

I followed her and listened as she listened and talked. "... Well, maybe he was just too busy... You sure?... Okay, I will. Bye!"

"That was Dad, right? What's going on?"

Mom headed for the living room, saying, "Sarge wouldn't tell him anything. Your father said he seemed miffed at him." She clicked on the TV. "He's on his way over to the police station now to try to figure out what's going on."

"You think there's something on the news?"

"Dad thinks we should check." She thumbed the remote until she found Chatty Adams's station.

"Mom? Shouldn't we be doing something? You know, about Mr. Green?"

"Mr. Green will be fine, Nolan. He hasn't done anything wrong."

"Do you think...do you think he'll tell?"

She looked at me. "Who Shredderman is?"

I nodded.

Very slowly, she shook her head. "No, I don't think he will."

I let out a sigh. "Phew."

"But I am wondering what you've gotten us all into, and how long you expect us to keep this up."

I just looked at her, feeling helpless. Why, oh why, did I ever tell them I was Shredderman?

Mom sighed and went back to looking at the TV. "There should be a news brief at the top of the hour. We'll see if they announce anything."

The news wasn't on yet. Some stupid show with people kissing was. Mom muted the sound, but that didn't really help. Boy! Were they ever kissing!

Mom turned the TV off for a minute, then turned it back on. They were *still* kissing.

Mom clicked it off.

We watched the clock.

She clicked it back on.

Phew! They were finally done kissing. But now the guy was leaving and the girl was crying! What kind of stupid show was this?

When it was finally over, Mom sighed and said, "Okay. They should have a few minutes of news now."

After a couple of commercials, the news brief started. A man behind a big desk said something about some senator being in trouble, some hurricane in Louisiana, and the president taking a trip to India. Then, at the very end, he said, "And for those of you who have been following the Shredderman story, we'll have late-breaking developments for you at five."

"At five!" I cried when he was done. "I can't wait two hours!"

Mom turned off the TV and said, "We'll see what your dad comes up with between now and then." She gave me a stern look. "In the meantime, you are banned from your computer, do you hear me?"

"But, Mo-om!"

"No!" She shot a finger my way. "You stay off of it!" She paced around a little, then said, "Look. Your favorite show's on in a little while. Watch some TV. The time will fly by."

I didn't want to watch TV!

Not even *The Gecko and Sticky*.

I wanted to know what was going on with Mr. Green!

Maybe I could ride over to the police station.

Maybe I could call Mr. Green!

Maybe I could—

"Nolan," Mom warned. "I can see you thinking

over there, and the answer is NO. You are going to stay right here. You are going to *wait* until we find out what's going on. And if that means I have to sit on you to hold you still, I will."

"But, Mo-om—"

She put her arm around my shoulders. "Nolan, I'm trying to protect you. You and Mr. Green and your father. I know it's hard, but sometimes the best thing to do is to do nothing at all." She smiled at me and clicked on the television. "How many times do I *make* you watch TV, huh?" She laughed. "Enjoy it while you can. I have some phone calls I have to make for work, so you just stay put and stay out of trouble, okay?"

I nodded. But the more I thought about it, the more I knew I couldn't just sit there watching TV. What kind of superhero hangs around watching cartoons while his ex-sidekick gets hauled off to the police station?

Not this one!

No way!

I moved around some throw pillows and a couch blanket so it sort of looked like I was lying on the couch.

My backpack was right there, so I took out supplies and wrote a note:

> Please don't be mad—I have to help
> Mr. Green!

I put it on top of my fake body, then strapped on my backpack and checked down the hallway.

The coast was clear.

So I tiptoed down to the garage, clipped on my helmet, and jumped on my bike.

It was time to find out what was going on.

CHAPTER 13
Cops at the Cabin

The fastest I'd ever gone on my bike before was 24.5 miles per hour. Not fast enough for a speeding ticket, but close!

But now, boy! My digital speedometer was clocking me at 25...26...26.5 miles per hour!

I was jumping curbs!

Cutting corners!

I was standing up, cranking the pedals like mad!

I zoomed over the Cedar Creek Bridge. Past Old Town!

I turned off the main road.

I turned onto a gravel road.

Then a dirt road!

Yes, I did know where I was going. Since Dad

had shown me the map, I knew exactly how to get to Mr. Green's cabin. And when those green logs came into view, I found out that my hunch was right—Mr. Green was in serious trouble. There were police cars. Black SUVs. Regular cars. And a white news van.

That doggone Chatty Adams was everywhere!

I saw Chatty talking to a policeman near the cabin. Even from across the woods, I could tell she was arguing with him. Finally she spun around and stormed back to the news van.

I decided to park my bike behind some trees and sneak in closer.

Nobody seemed to notice me, and I got so close to Chatty and her crew that I could hear them talking.

"I think we've got enough to break the story," Chatty was saying.

A man with a short gray beard was looking at some papers, shaking his head. "We can go with

the opening segment here, but a lot of the rest of this is speculation. We can't guess, Chatty, we have to know."

"Oh, come on, Roy! All fingers point to this Green guy." She snatched the papers from him and said, "Look, we know the documents were classified. You've said yourself that I have a nose for these things, and what I smell here is a traitor! A man selling his country's secrets to the enemy.

And come on—you saw him! He's got 'rebel' written all over him." She motioned toward his house. "Who lives out in the boonies in a green log cabin, for cryin' out loud? I bet he's one of these guys who hates the government and has an arsenal of guns stashed in there!"

Guns?

Was she *crazy*?

Mr. Green didn't have a bunch of guns.

He had a bunch of guitars!

And why did they think he was selling secrets to the enemy? If they were talking about the papers I'd sent to Sarge, they didn't have anything to *do* with Mr. Green!

The Roy guy was still shaking his head. "I know you think your source is reliable—"

"They're inside the police department!"

"I still want to hold off until we can confirm some things. A lot of what you've got just isn't adding up."

Chatty rolled her eyes and let out a big sigh. "We're gonna get scooped on this. You see that guy over there right now, chumming it up with the cops? You see him? Huh?"

"That's the local news guy, Chatty. His name's Harry Kane. He was recently bumped up from weatherman—believe me, he's no threat."

"Well, why do they kick me out and let him in?"

"Take it easy, Chatty. They're probably just shooting the breeze. Remember: he's small-time, you're big-time. In the end, people always want to see themselves on national TV."

"But I want to break the story! It's mine, you hear me? Mine!"

"I know it is, sweetheart," he said, trying to calm her down. "And you will. Right now, why don't we shoot that opening segment. It's a good start."

Chatty sighed. "This moss-minded town is driving me nuts!"

"I know it is, sweetheart. Now let's go."

A few minutes later they had the camera set up and Chatty was looking straight into it, saying, "What do classified documents, a one-hundred-thousand-dollar payoff, and Shredderman have in common? A fifth-grade elementary school teacher, that's what. Elmo Green, who lives in this cabin in the woods in Cedar Valley, California, was taken in for questioning today after footprints led authorities from the site of an alleged espionage operation to Mr. Green's front door."

Footprints?

Oh, no!

I'd led the police right to Mr. Green!

Chatty was still talking. "Authorities found out about the cash-for-secrets exchange when the Cedar Valley police force received a cryptic message from the mysterious 'Shredderman.' They were able to discern the location of the exchange from attached photographs, but it is still unclear whether Elmo Green is being questioned as Shredderman, or for possible involvement in selling national secrets, or both. The local police chief has confirmed that since this is a matter of national security, federal agents are now involved."

Federal agents?

The FBI?

And she said "national security"!

Uh-quintuple-oh!

My heart was beating like crazy.

The FBI would be able to find out who owned the Shredderman site!

I had to get home!

Fast!

CHAPTER 14
The FBI

I did ride fast—25...26...27.5 miles an hour!

But it wasn't fast enough.

As I rounded the corner and came down our street, I spotted a black SUV parked in front of my house. It looked a lot like one of the cars that had been in front of Mr. Green's cabin!

I slowed, then cut into the school, which was pretty much deserted. I left my bike out of view, then took the binoculars out of my backpack and crawled around bushes until I could see my house.

I looked through my binoculars. The SUV didn't say "FBI" on it or anything, but I could tell by the man standing next to it that it was an FBI vehicle. Partly it was the way he was standing by the car, looking at everything like a hawk. Mostly it was the way he was dressed. His hair looked like it had been cut by an FBI barber.

His pants looked like they'd come straight from the FBI store!

And his sunglasses were black-black. Sleek. Definitely FBI-issue shades!

All of a sudden the front door to my house opened.

Another FBI guy came out!

And another!

They were carrying a computer!

I focused on it as they hauled it to the car. It wasn't my computer—it was my mom's! And right behind them, with her hand wrapped around my mother's arm, was an FBI lady!

They were taking my mother away?

Why?

I focused the binoculars on my mother's face. She seemed serious, but she wasn't crying. She was just going along, getting in the back of the

SUV. And before I could run home and yell "Let her go!" they were driving her away.

I jumped on my bike and chased after them. As fast as I could, as hard as I could, I pedaled after that SUV! And boy, it's a good thing there are red lights! It gave me the chance to catch up while they waited for them to turn green.

We were getting near the Cedar Creek Bridge when a news van came blasting over it, going the opposite direction. Chatty Adams was in the passenger seat!

I looked over my shoulder as they zoomed by. Was she going to our house?

Had she heard they were arresting my mom?

But Chatty Adams must have spotted the SUV, because all of a sudden the news van spun a U-turn!

It was coming after us!

Was Chatty going to yell a bunch of questions at my mom?

Was my mom going to be on national TV?

Were they going to make her seem like a criminal?

If Chatty could, she would!

I moved over from the right side of the road and rode smack-dab in the *middle* of the bridge. I had to stop Chatty Adams! She was crazy! She thought Mr. Green had a house full of guns! Who knew what she'd say about my mom!

Chatty's van honked.

I kept riding in the middle of the road, pretending I didn't hear.

The van honked longer. Louder!

I kept riding in the middle of the road, *doity-doity-doity-doy.*

When we were over the bridge, the van went off the road, onto the shoulder! It guzzled gas like crazy as it passed me by! Chatty Adams glared out the window at me.

I pretended I didn't see her. *Doity-doity-doity-doy.*

But now I had to catch up again! And boy, they were going so fast!

I tried my hardest, but I just couldn't keep up. There was a long stretch of road with no stoplights, and they lost me.

When I got to Old Town, I skidded to a halt at a pay phone. I dug through my backpack for leftover lunch money. My legs were shaky from the ride. And my head was pouring sweat! I tore off my helmet and dropped coins into the pay phone. My hands were shaking as I punched in my mother's cell phone number.

Brrrring . . . brrrring . . . brrrr . . .

"Hello?"

"Mom! I saw them taking you away."

"Calm down, Nolan. I'm fine," she said to me. Then, to someone else, she snapped, "Do you mind? It's my son. He's worried."

I guess they decided to let her talk to me, because she said, "Everything's going to be okay, honey."

"They took your computer," I whispered. *"Why?"*

"They seem to think I'm Shredderman," she said. *"You?"*

She laughed. "Pretty funny, huh?" Then she added, "By the way, they've taken your dad in for questioning, too."

My dad, too! Oh, no! They had him, my mom, and Mr. Green? What had I *done?*

"Mom, I'm sorry I took off. I had to—"

"We'll sort this all out later, okay? Right now, you just stay safe. Everything will be fine. Your father and I haven't done anything wrong. They just want to ask us a few questions down at the police station. But since we haven't done anything *wrong*, we're not in any *trouble*, okay?"

She was being so calm. She sounded so... *brave*. "Mom?" I asked, and boy, my voice was quivering! "What should I do?"

"Where are you?"

"In Old Town. At a pay phone."

"Go home, Nolan. Go home and wait. I'll call you there when we're done. It shouldn't be too long," she added cheerfully, "seeing how I don't know anything about Shredderman."

"You rock, Mom!"

She laughed, and I could tell she was going to hang up, so real quick I said, "By the way, Chatty Adams is right behind you."

"Oh, brother," she said. Then she started to ask, "How did you...?" but stopped herself. "Never mind. I'll talk to you soon, okay, honey?"

"Okay," I said, and hung up. Then I picked up my bike and clipped on my helmet.

Shredderman had work to do!

CHAPTER 15
Holy Cryptanalysis, Batman!

The police station's not that far from Old Town. If I'd have gone straight there instead of stopping to call my mom, I might even have beat them. There are lots of stoplights along the way that

would have slowed the FBI down. Stoplights I was now running!

But by the time I got to the police station, Mom was nowhere to be found. Lots of other people were on the police station steps and around the parking lot, though. There were even a few kids from my class, probably trying to find out what was happening to Mr. Green. I saw Ian McCoy and his friend Vinnie. Trey was there, talking to Marvin Speltz. And there were some girls, too. Miriam and Danielle and Trinity. And uh-oh...

Bubba.

Bubba Bixby hadn't given me trouble for a while, but he still made me nervous! Then

Miriam spotted me. And she nudged Trinity, who nudged Danielle, and pretty soon there was this whole chain reaction and everyone was charging over to me.

"Hey!" Marvin said. "I heard they arrested your *parents*."

"They did not!" I said, wishing I had gone home.

"Uh-huh!" Vinnie said. "That dude over there said they've arrested Eve and Steven Byrd. Those are *your* parents, Nerd, in case you didn't know it."

"Shut up," I told him. "They didn't *arrest* them, they just want to ask them a few questions."

"Nuh-uh, dude! The FBI hauled 'em in for treason!" Marvin said.

"Who told you that?" I demanded.

"That news reporter dude. You know..." He pointed over by the station steps. "What's-his-face."

"Harry Kane," Miriam said. "He used to do the weather, but now he does news. My parents watch him every night."

Boy, did I have a thing or two to say to Harry Kane! I parked my bike and power-walked right up to him. And to my surprise, all my classmates followed.

Nobody ever follows me—they usually avoid me!

But I guess they were curious about what was going on with my mom and dad, so they all tagged along. By the time I got up to Harry Kane, I felt like I had a whole army behind me!

Not that they would *defend* me or anything, but still, it made me feel more sure about what I was going to tell him.

"Hey," Harry said. He was leaning on the wooden railing by the steps, chewing on a toothpick. "What's up?"

"My name's Nolan Byrd," I told him. "My parents are Eve and Steven Byrd."

"Ah," he said with a little smile. His toothpick was like a skinny wooden fang, sticking straight out.

"My parents are not traitors or spies or anything

else. They're good guys! And," I added, "so is Mr. Green."

"I see," he said, but he was still kind of grinning.

"Mr. Kane, I'm serious! They had nothing to do with any of this, and I don't think you should go around telling people they've committed treason when they haven't!"

A guy with a big camera came up and aimed it at me, but Harry yanked the toothpick out of his mouth and pointed it at the camera guy like a micro magic wand. "No, man," he said. "Not the kid."

"But, Harry…"

"I said no, man. It's not cool." He kept pointing the toothpick right at him until the cameraman grumbled, "Whatever," and backed off.

Harry turned to me and said, "I know your dad—not real well, but I do know him. We've covered a lot of the same stories—him for the paper, me for TV. Always seemed like a pretty decent guy to me—"

"He *is*. He's a great guy! So's my mom!"

He scratched his neck and looked at me. "You said your name's Nolan, right?"

I nodded.

"Okay, Nolan, I'll tell you what. I'll do my best to be sensitive to what you're going through, but if your parents are part of an international spy ring, it's my job to report it."

An international spy ring? Holy cryptanalysis, Batman! This was getting bigger by the minute!

"You've got it all wrong! My parents aren't the spies! Neither is Mr. Green! They're the *good* guys!"

"That's right," a few of the kids said. "No way is Mr. Green a spy."

"Yeah!" said Vinnie. "He's a hippie!"

Harry laughed. "Well, look. I appreciate that you kids are sticking up for your teacher and Nolan's parents, but like I said—"

I interrupted him. "How would *you* like to be plastered all over the news as a criminal when you were the good guy? My parents and Mr. Green are the good guys, I *promise* you."

"All right, all right! I said I'd be sensitive, okay? My sources are telling me that none of them is being very forthcoming—"

"Whaddaya mean, 'forthcoming'?" Vinnie asked.

"You know—they're all keeping their mouths shut." Harry leaned forward a little. "That usually means they're *hiding* something."

Maybe, but it wasn't *spy* information!

"But—" I said.

"*But*," he said, "I'll make sure the story's solid

before I run it. If they're spies, though, there's nothing I can do about that." He nodded over my shoulder at the parking lot. "Your real problem's not me, though. Your real problem's out there."

I looked over at the white news van parked under some trees. "You mean Chatty Adams?" I asked.

He nodded. "Good luck getting *that* news chick to back off." He snorted. "Just from the few days I've known her, I can promise you that she'll report what she's got, no matter who it hurts."

All of us were looking at Chatty now. And inside me I felt something strange swelling up. Something strong. Something I've only ever felt when I was being Shredderman.

But here I was, just Nolan Byrd, surrounded by classmates who were waiting. Waiting for *me* to say something. Or *do* something.

"Come on," I said, leading the way. "Let's go have a little chat with Chatty Adams!"

CHAPTER 16
Chatting with Chatty

They followed me. Every single one of my classmates followed me. Even Bubba Bixby! And on
the way over, Trinity whispered, "I like the way
you stood up for your parents, Nolan."

I didn't understand why she was whispering. Or
what the big deal was. "My parents are great," I
told her.

She nodded. "Mine are, too." She was still
whispering. "But it's not real cool to admit it, you
know what I mean?"

I couldn't help pulling a face. "Why?"

She smiled at me. "That's what I like about you,
Nolan." Then she scurried away to walk with
Miriam and Danielle.

Weird! But I didn't have time to think about it. I had to get my digital camera set up without anyone noticing, and I had to do it *while* I was walking!

This was going to take subtlety.

Finesse!

Some real legerdemain!

And believe me, I'm not known for my smooth moves.

Lucky for me, my camera was already in the secret compartment in my backpack. But I had to open the lens flap.

Get out the remote control.

Activate the camera and stash the remote in my sweatshirt pocket.

And I had to do it all without anyone asking me what I was doing!

First step, trip!

I'm good at tripping.

Comes real natural, believe me.

Turns out, I'm good at faking it, too. I pretended to stumble and twisted out of my backpack. And while I was recovering, I ripped open the lens flap, snuck the remote control in my pocket, and untied my shoe.

"You okay?" Trinity asked.

"Yeah," I muttered. "What a klutz, huh?"

"It's okay," she said with a smile. "When I do that, my mom says I'm just trying to catch up with a growth spurt." She pointed. "Look! You probably just tripped on your shoelace."

I tied it quick and picked up my backpack by the top loop, like a briefcase. "Thanks," I told her. Trinity really is pretty nice.

Then I noticed something amazing. All the other kids were waiting for me, too. They weren't hovering over me or anything, but they *were* waiting.

So I smiled at them and said, "Sorry! Klutz attack!"

They laughed. And for the first time ever, them laughing at me wasn't painful.

It felt good.

Like it was...okay that I was the way I was.

Like somewhere inside they actually *liked* me.

It was a very strange feeling.

A good feeling!

Actually, I felt about six feet tall! And by the time the group of us was at the news van, I felt really brave. If Chatty Adams didn't leave my parents and Mr. Green alone, boy, was she going to be sorry!

Chatty and that Roy guy had their backs to us. Roy was by the driver's door, talking on one cell phone. Chatty was by the passenger door, chattin' on another.

Maybe they were talking to each other!

How stupid would that be?

More likely, they were trying to get information about Mr. Green and my parents!

Chatty's camera guy was pulling equipment out of the van. He stopped working when he saw us and said, "Hey. What's up?"

"We're here to talk to Chatty," I said.

"You want autographs?"

"Not exactly," I said. "I have information."

His eyebrows went up.

"About . . . ?"

"The international spy ring." Man! Was I being cool, or what?

"Hey, Chatty!" he called. When she turned, the cameraman said, "They say they've got information."

She took one look at us and scowled at him.

He shrugged at her like, Don't blame me! and she turned her back on us, shaking her head.

So I went right up to her and said, "Excuse me, but this is important."

She looked at me like I was an annoying bug in her no-fly zone. "Go *away*."

"No," I said, loud and clear.

My classmates gasped.

Chatty's nose flared.

Her eyes squinted!

She was practically foaming at the mouth!

Finally she whispered "Call me back in five" into the phone and snapped it closed. She looked me over. Hair to toe. Toe to hair. Then she said, "So what do you want?"

"I want you to back off Mr. Green and the Byrds," I told her. "They're not spies, and they're not Shredderman—"

"I recognize you now!" Chatty was squinting at me but good. "You're that nerdy little kid from the elementary school who—"

"I am *not* nerdy," I told her.

"Yeah," someone beside me growled. "He's just smart."

I recognized the voice, but I still couldn't believe my eyes when I turned and saw who'd said it.

Bubba Bixby.

None of my other classmates could believe it, either. For a second no one said anything. But

then all at once, other kids started shouting stuff at Chatty.

"Why you callin' him names?"

"Yeah! He hasn't done anything to you!"

"Yeah, lady. If you call him anything, call him *Mister*."

"Yeah! 'Cause one of these days, *you'll* be working for *him*."

Now I couldn't believe my *ears*. These were my classmates. The same kids who'd been calling me Nerd for years!

"What *is* this?" Chatty said, still squinting away. "Roy!" she called over her shoulder. "Get these stupid kids *out* of here!"

"Look," I said. "We're not trying to bother you—"

"Well, you're doing a pretty good job of it, anyway!"

"We're just here to ask you to leave the Byrds and Mr. Green alone. They're innocent."

"Oh, yeah? Well, how would you know?"

"I know because—"

But before I could say more, she said through a smirk, "And what are you gonna do if I don't, huh? Sic your *calculator* on me?"

"Hey!" Trinity said. "That's cold!"

"Yeah!" Ian yelled. "Why don't you *listen* to him?"

But she wasn't about to. We were just kids. Annoying little kids.

Little did she know that Shredderman was a kid!

I moved my backpack so the camera was angled at Chatty. From the look on her face, I could tell that with one more little nudge it would be showtime!

I reached inside my pocket and pressed the camera's remote control.

Movie mode, go!

And then good ol' Vinnie shouted, "Yeah! What's your problem?"

And...action!

"My problem?" Chatty said, winding up. "My *problem* is you, you twerp." She started pointing around, picking on us one at a time. "And you, you geek! And you, you wannabe Barbie! And you, you big-beak brat! And you, you fatso! And especially *you*, you annoying knuckleheaded *nerd*. Can't you tell I'm busy? Get *away* from me!"

"Whoa-whoa-whoa-whoa-*whoa*." Roy was pulling her away, trying to calm her down. "Easy, sweetheart. It's okay. Everything's ooooookay." Then he called over to us, "I'm sorry about that, kids. She didn't mean any of that. She's just under a lot of pressure."

But then Chatty spotted a police car zooming across the parking lot.

Her eyes got sharp.

Her nostrils flared.

She wrestled free from Roy and started moving like a barracuda after blood.

"They've got someone else!" she cried to her cameraman. "Come on!"

The rest of us ran after the police car, too. And when we caught up, I saw that Chatty was right. They *did* have someone in the backseat.

Someone I recognized!

CHAPTER 17
Sweating Bullets

Harry Kane got to the police car about the same time Chatty and the rest of us did. Chatty shoved Harry aside and shouted, "Can you tell us who you've got there?"

Two policemen had pulled their prisoner out of the backseat. It was the shabby guy who had left the papers in the boulder and taken the money!

He was handcuffed!

"What is he charged with?" Chatty shouted. "Is this one of the international spies?"

Both the policemen shook their heads, telling her they weren't going to answer her questions.

She chased after them anyway. "Is he Shredderman?"

Shredderman? How could she think *that?* Shredderman had blown the whistle on this guy!

How stupid could this lady be?

One of the police officers seemed to be thinking the same thing, because he stopped in his tracks and gave her a long, steady look. Then he let the other policeman take their prisoner into the station while he stayed outside. He came a few steps our way, then cleared his throat and said, "I understand that you've got a lot of questions concerning this case, and we *will* answer them to the best of our ability when the time is right—"

"When will *that* be?" Chatty snapped. "You expect us to wait out here all night?"

The policeman took a deep breath. "How about we give you a statement in...oh, half an hour?"

"Can't you give us *any*thing now? Who is that man? Why was he arrested? Are you going to—"

Harry cut in. "Hey, Don, can you tell us if this arrest means you'll be releasing the Byrds and

Elmo Green?" He glanced at us. "There are some people here who'd really like to know."

"Hi, Harry," the policeman answered. "I'd like to help you on that, but right now I can't say. Someone'll be back out in half an hour, okay?"

"Good enough, Don," Harry said.

"Hey, Don!" Chatty called.

The policeman put up a hand before she could say anything more. "Please, Ms. Adams. That's enough. I'll have someone back here in half an hour."

Chatty practically stomped her foot. Then she stormed off, muttering, "Bunch of good ol' boys around here. Bunch of lousy, clubfooted good ol' boys."

Roy was on her again, saying, "Chatty, knock it off! You've scared off your source, and now you're alienating this whole town!"

"But it's not right! I was here first! This is *my* story!"

"It's still your story, Chatty. Calm down!"

"No, it's not! You think they're gonna keep a lid on this? You watch. In half an hour, this place will be swarming with reporters!"

Chatty stormed off to her news van, and I was expecting my classmates to take off, too, but they didn't. Trinity said, "I'm going to call my mom, but I'll wait with you, okay, Nolan?"

"Me too," Ian said, then looked at Vinnie. "You taking off?"

"No way." He was walking backward quick, with one eye on Trinity. "I'm just gonna beat Pony-girl to the phone!" She tried to punch him, but he took off running.

Some kids called home on their cell phones. Some went to the pay phone. I didn't have to call anyone—my parents were in the police station.

Maybe even in jail!

Someone else didn't call his parents, either.

Bubba.

And the way he was acting was making me nervous.

He was quiet.

Very quiet.

And he was watching me, kind of pacing back and forth.

Like he was thinking.

No, more like stalking prey.

But he hadn't given me trouble in weeks. Weeks and weeks! Ever since I'd done him a great big—make that *enormous*—favor.

But still. Right now, he was looking very...*dangerous*.

I tried to wave at him, like, Hey, dude. What's happening? But it was a pretty lame wave, even I could tell.

And it made him do the one thing I *didn't* want him to do.

Walk my way.

Uh-oh. Was he going to pound me?

But why would he?

Unless he...unless he sus-pected that *I* was the one who'd posted his Big Butt on the World Wide Web. Unless he'd figured out that *I* was the one who'd gotten him busted for bullying. Unless he'd figured out that *I* was...

Shredderman.

Kids were starting to move our way. But before anyone got there, Bubba came right up to me and said, "I'm not as dumb as you think."

I gulped. "Who said you were dumb?"

"I know that's what you think."

Actually, I didn't think that. Bubba had managed to get through *years* of bullying and stealing and lying. Sure, I thought he was sneaky, but you can't be dumb and get away with all of that.

I shook my head. "I don't think you're—"

"I can put two and two together, man."

"You can multiply them, too! And divide them! And probably even exponentiate them!" Man, my *mouth* was the one that was dumb. Real quick, I added, "I didn't mean that the way it sounded. Honest!"

"Just *listen* to me, Nolan."

At least he wasn't back to calling me Nerd. I gulped and nodded.

"You humiliated me, dude. All those jokes about me. That picture of my butt. I swore when I figured it out I'd beat whoever it was to a pulp."

I was sweating bullets.

He knew!

Without a doubt, Bubba Bixby knew.

Other kids were coming in closer. And closer. He was going to say it! He was going to blow my cover.

How could he resist?

Bubba looked around at all the kids gathered. He was feeling the power of it! The glory of it!

This was it—I was about to be unmasked.

And by Bubba Bixby!

He looked right at me. There was a hint of a smile on his face. He cocked his nose, like, Come here.

I squinted a little, like, Huh?

He did it again, then said to everyone else, "Step back! I gotta ask Nolan something."

Everyone backed up, boy! Nobody could figure out *what* was going on, but they sure didn't want to be in the middle of it!

Then Bubba said to me, "Come *here*, dude!"

What else could I do? I moved a step forward.

He rolled his eyes.

I moved another step closer.

He grabbed my arm and yanked me next to him.

But he didn't pound me.

He didn't hurl me onto the pavement.

No, instead, he *whispered* in my ear.

And what he said was, "You need a sidekick, man?"

CHAPTER 18
A New Sidekick

"I'm serious, dude," he whispered when I took a step back. "I'd be good!" He flexed an arm and grinned at me. "I kinda look like the Bouncer, don't you think?"

I was just staring at him, my mind going a million miles an hour.

He knew. There was no doubt about it.

But Bubba Bixby as the *Bouncer*? Bubba was the whole reason I put on the Shredderman mask in the first place. And now he wanted to be my sidekick?

But what if I said no? What would he do then? Pound me?

Or worse—unmask me?

Bubba put down his arm and said, "You're thinking this is a threat, aren't you?"

I just stared at him.

"Well, it's not, dude. I just think it'd be cool."

I kept right on staring. My whole face felt frozen in place!

He sighed. "Man, you're thinking I'm going to rat you off, aren't you? Well, I'm not the creep you think I am. And to prove it, I tell you what— whether you say I can be the Bouncer or not, I ain't squealin'. Now or ever. You got my word."

His *word*? Bubba Bixby's word was about as good as a punctured ink cartridge!

But I couldn't just keep standing there, staring! I had to say *some*thing! Bubba had figured it out, and I could see he wasn't just guessing.

He *knew*.

But Bubba Bixby as a sidekick?

I practically laughed out loud.

It was just too . . . ironic.

Paradoxical!

Totally unexpected!

Completely surprising!

My face thawed into a little smile, and I heard myself whisper, "I wasn't aware that you were big on truth and justice. But there *does* happen to be an opening."

He pumped his arm and said, "Yes!" Then he whispered, "And, dude, I can totally get into truth and justice. Wait and see. I'm gonna be the best—"

"*Shhhhh-shhh-shhh!*"

Kids were sneaking in closer.

"Oh. Oh, right," Bubba said. He put on a poker face. "I'm cool. I'm cool."

Trinity was the first to say something. "You okay, Nolan?"

"Yeah," I said, and tossed a look at Bubba. "Everything's cool, right?"

"Absolutely!" Bubba was grinning from ear to ear. "Everything is way cool." Then he laughed and said, "It's nifty. Groovy! Awesome! You might even say it's *copacetic*."

Everyone busted up. And I knew they were laughing because Bubba was doing what *I* always do, but he wasn't really making fun of me.

It was just funny!

"Copacetic, dude?" Vinnie called. "Can you *spell* that, too?"

"Yeah, man!" Bubba called back. "It's spelled C-O-O-L."

Everyone laughed again.

Then Trey came charging up, all out of breath. "Hey, guys! Have you seen that crowd on the steps? It's, like, twice as big as it was before!"

We looked over, and wow! People seemed to be pouring in from everywhere!

"Chatty Adams is gonna be so ticked!" Danielle said. "Two other news vans just showed up!"

By the time half an hour was up, you couldn't even see the station steps. They were packed with people! Cameras! Someone even set up a podium and put microphones around it!

Then they rolled out some CAUTION tape that we weren't allowed to cross.

The place was buzzing with gossip!

Cedar Valley had never seen anything like this!

A lot more kids from school showed up, too. Some with parents, some without. We kids all hung together, and pretty soon we were spotting *teachers* from our school.

"There's Mrs. Bernhart!"

"And Miss Simms!"

"There's Miss Surkit!"

"And look! There's Mr. Hoover!" Marvin

Speltz cried. "I tell you, guys—janitor by day, Shredderman by night. That's why he's here!"

"Don't be a doof," Mike McDermish told him.

Miriam interrupted them. "Look! There's Dr. Voss! Even our *principal* is here!"

Half an hour grew into an hour. Chatty Adams spent half her time yelling into her cell phone and the other half snapping at Roy and her cameraman. She was trying to keep people away from "her" area, and boy, was she being mean!

Then I got an idea. And I started wondering— was a news camera like the video camera we had at home?

I couldn't see a power source.

Did it run on batteries?

Chatty's cameraman was standing pretty close to her. His camera was resting on the pavement by his feet

I snuck over.

If only I had an invisibility cloak.

Or a magic Aztec wristband!

If only I could get in close enough to . . .

Chatty noticed me and yelled, "Scram! You hear me? Get *away* from this area! You have no business being here whatsoever! I said scram!"

Drat! How was I ever going to . . . Then I noticed that the guy from another news station had a camera just like Chatty's.

I inched my way over to it.

He was holding it by its handle, alongside his leg.

"Pretty cool rig, huh?" he said when he saw me checking it out.

"Sure is. Looks heavy, though."

He shrugged. "You get used to it."

"How's it powered? Batteries?"

"Yup." He hefted it and pointed. "Right here."

"That's it? That powers this whole camera?"

"Well, the battery goes way inside." He pressed a lever and pulled it out. "See?"

It was big!

"And when this one gets low, I've got a backup right here." He popped the backup off the camera, where it was stored. "See? Two seconds is all it takes to swap them, and I'm good to go."

"Wow," I told him. "That is one cool camera." He let me look it over for a minute, so I said, "Thanks for being so nice."

He grinned and said, "No problem." He shot a look at Chatty and dropped his voice. "Besides, I saw how that prima donna was treating you. Believe me, she's not anyone's favorite."

Just then, the police station door opened.

A man in a suit and tie came out.

A man in a uniform came out right behind him! Was that...Sergeant Klubb?

It was!

Photographers all around hoisted their cameras.

All the reporters jockeyed for position.

The men from the station were moving slowly toward the podium.

I raced over to Bubba and whispered, "*Pssst!* I need your help." I pulled him over to the side.

"As the Bouncer?" he whispered.

I nodded. "See Chatty's cameraman?"

He looked over at him. "Yeah?"

"I need you to bump him. Hard."

"You want me to bring him down?" Bubba whispered. "I can land that dude, easy."

"No! Just distract him so I can pop the battery pack out of his camera."

"But why? There's all these other news guys here."

Why did my sidekicks always argue with me? I frowned at him. "Because Chatty Adams is not here for truth or justice. She's here for herself."

He nodded slowly and said, "Got it," but I could tell he didn't.

"Besides," I whispered as we hurried over, "didn't you hear her call you 'fatso' back there?"

"Hey! That's right!"

"You think I'm gonna let someone call my side-kick 'fatso'?"

For a second his face went blank. Then a light seemed to come on inside him. He grinned at me and said, "Dude, you really do shred!"

And with that, Bubba Bixby *charged*.

CHAPTER 19
Charge!

I know from experience that when Bubba wants
to bring someone down, he brings them *down*.
Chatty's cameraman didn't have a chance.

"Oh, dude! I'm so sorry!" Bubba said. He
helped him up, then "accidentally" tripped and
knocked him over again.

POW!

Meanwhile, I was zeroing in on the camera.

I got my hands on the battery.

The camera twisted away!

I got my hands on it again, and *click, thwack!* Battery number one was mine!

Boy! Was it heavy!

I held it between my knees and...

Click, thwack!

I pulled off the backup battery!

Lucky for me, Chatty was too busy being pushy to pay attention to what was going on.

The cameraman was back on his feet now.

Bubba was dusting him off!

So far, Bubba the Bouncer rocked!

He looked my way and I gave him a nod.

Mission accomplished!

We raced back over to the rest of the kids. "Stay cool," I told him as I stashed the batteries in my backpack and strapped the backpack on. "Stay totally cool."

He nodded, but he was anything *but* cool. He was amped, and panting like crazy!

After he caught his breath, he whispered, "I am *lovin'* this! So now what?"

"So now we listen," I whispered.

"We *listen?*" Bubba whispered back.

"*Shhhhh!*" I warned. "I've got to find out what's going on."

"Good evening," the man in the suit and tie said, holding on to the podium with both hands while Sarge stood off to one side. "As many of you know, I'm Scott Yardland, Cedar Valley's chief of police. Unfortunately, our bucolic community—"

"Bucolic? What's that?" Bubba whispered.

"Lots of trees," I whispered back.

"—has apparently been home to the maneuverings of an international spy ring."

"Have you apprehended the spies?" Chatty Adams shouted.

"If you'll *please* be patient," Chief Yardland

said, giving her a hard look, "we'll get to that."
He went back to his speech. "Please understand
that we're in the middle of a very complex and
delicate situation. There are things we are not yet
at liberty to disclose—"

"Disclose?" Bubba whispered.

"Tell us about," I whispered back. "There are
things he can't tell us about."

"—but what I *can* tell you is that we have arrested
one individual and have detained three others, all
connected to a cash-for-secrets exchange that we
believe took place under the Blackstone Way
Bridge. Unfortunately, *none* of the individuals in
custody is cooperating with authorities. I can also
tell you that the arrested man has been positively
ID'd as the individual we suspect of selling the
highly sensitive classified documents."

"What is the nature of the documents?" a lady
with a notepad called out.

Chief Yardland gave her a friendly little smirk.

"That they're classified. Top-secret."

"Military?" another reporter asked.

"The FBI has asked me not to discuss specifics. I am not at liberty to say anything more about the documents at this time."

All of a sudden, there was a big commotion across the crowd from us. Chatty's arms were flying in the air as she yelled at her cameraman. Then she started yelling at Roy!

I grinned at Bubba.

Bubba grinned at me.

We slapped a sly-five on each other and watched as Chatty zoomed around, trying to bum a battery off other cameramen.

"How about the other people you've detained?" a reporter shouted at the chief. "You've got a woman, her husband, and a teacher in custody, is that right?"

"Yes. They have not been charged with anything yet. Our initial impression was that they were only involved peripherally—"

"Peripherally?" Bubba whispered.

"On the edge. Only a little," I whispered back, wishing Chief Yardland would stop using such big words.

"—but it's clear that they are holding back information. We'll see what transpires over the next few hours."

"Transpires?" Bubba whispered.

"Happens," I whispered back.

"Why doesn't he just *say* that?"

I shrugged. "Good question."

"What's the Shredderman connection?" Harry Kane called out.

The chief sighed. "Shredderman is the one who brought the money-for-secrets situation to our attention. At first we thought he was assisting law enforcement. We now believe he—or *she*, or *they*—may be someone with an axe to grind. Someone who was once part of the spy ring and is now on the outs."

"You're crazy!" I shouted.

People nearby stared at me.

Oops!

Bubba whispered, "Stay cool, dude, remember?"

But how could they think that? How could they possibly think that?

The chief went on. "Regardless, our three detainees will either be released if they answer questions to the FBI's satisfaction or be arrested on charges of conspiracy and obstruction of justice."

Arrested for conspiracy!

Obstruction of justice!

No!

"No, no, no, no!" I didn't even know I was shouting it out loud. Bubba tried to hold me back, but I twisted free and pushed through the crowd. These were my parents! My teacher! They were the best friends I'd ever had.

How could I let them be arrested for obstruction of *justice*?

They weren't answering questions because they were protecting my secret identity! I could see them now, under a hot, bare bulb, being grilled by the FBI! Being tortured with questions they wouldn't answer because of me! All because I'd been so stubborn about fighting for truth and justice.

Well, what kind of truth and justice was *this*?

They were going to go to *jail* because of me!

"You're wrong!" I shouted. I ducked under the yellow CAUTION tape and cried, "You're completely wrong!"

Chief Yardland said something about removing me from the area, but Sarge stepped in and said, "It's okay, Chief. This is the Byrds' son. He's just upset."

"I am *not* just upset!" I shouted.

Boy, did I ever sound upset!

But I kept right on shouting. "They're not spies! They don't have an axe to grind! They didn't have anything to do with *any* of this!"

The chief was looking at me like he felt so, *so* sorry for me. Like I was just a poor little kid who didn't understand how the real world worked.

I looked around at the crowd.

Everyone was thinking the same thing as Chief Yardland: Poor kid...his parents are spies.

"They're not spies, and they're not Shredderman!" I looked at the crowd. At all the cameras aimed my way. At all the people staring at me. At the kids from my school and the teachers and my principal.

Sarge put his arm around my shoulders and tried to pull me aside, saying, "Now, Nolan..."

I twisted away from him and shouted, "I know for a *fact* they're not spies! And I know for a *fact* they're not Shredderman! I know because..."

The crowd fell quiet.

I could hear the breeze sweep through tree branches.

Pine needles seemed to fall in slow motion.

Everything seemed a little fuzzy.

Soft.

"Because . . . ?" Sarge prompted.

I took a deep breath, and slowly everything came into focus.

So I turned to face the crowd and said it loud.

Said it strong!

"I know, because *I'm* Shredderman!"

I'm SHREDDERMAN!

CHAPTER 20
Shred-der-man!

The crowd didn't gasp.

There wasn't even a moment of stunned silence.

No, people *giggled*.

And *groaned*.

And said, "Oh, poor kid."

"But I *am*," I shouted. I swung my backpack off. "And I can prove it!"

People were rolling their eyes.

Tisking their tongues!

The chief was trying to get Sarge to drag me away, but I whipped out my digital camera and scanned back through the pictures I'd taken of the spies and the phony boulder.

"Look!" I said to Sarge. "This is proof! Who else would have these shots?"

Sarge's jaw dropped as I thumbed through the pictures. "Scott!" he said to the chief. "Look at these!"

When Chief Yardland was hanging over my shoulder, too, I said, "The FBI traced Shredderman to my house, but they took the wrong

computer. Everything's on *my* computer. It's in my bedroom."

People were starting to whisper.

"My parents and Mr. Green are trying to protect me, that's all. They don't have anything to do with this! Actually, they're pretty *mad* about it! And if you still don't believe me, I can tell you what's in those classified documents! Not what they *mean* or anything, but they're twelve pages of calculations and diagrams of—"

"Enough!" Chief Yardland said. "I believe you!"

Now everyone was talking a hundred miles an hour! The crowd sounded like a giant computer, buzzing for an Internet connection.

Dr. Voss had moved to the front of the crowd. She yelled, "And Mr. Green's the Bouncer, isn't he? I knew it all along!"

I froze. Dr. Voss would fire him!

But before I could figure out what to say, Bubba Bixby came tripping over the CAUTION tape, yelling, "Mr. Green's not the Bouncer! I am!"

"*You?*" Dr. Voss looked from Bubba to me, and back again.

I practically laughed out loud.

I didn't have to explain anything!

Or lie!

It was the truth!

And boy, did it seem just.

"But that doesn't make any *sense*," Dr. Voss cried. "You *hate* each other!"

"Well," I said, putting my hand on my new sidekick's shoulder. "The truth is that Bubba here *is* the Bouncer."

Bubba squared his shoulders.

He stuck his chin forward a little.

Then he cleared his throat and said, "I was only involved *peripherally* with what *transpired*—a fact I didn't want to *disclose* in this *bucolic* setting—but it's true." He made a muscleman pose with his arms and cried, "I *am* the Bouncer!"

The kids from school all dropped their jaws. They were in total shock over everything!

Except for Trinity. She was bouncing up and down, clapping like crazy. She saw me looking her way and blew me a kiss.

A *kiss*.

Do superheroes blush?

This one sure did!

How embarrassing!

Then the questions started flying at us: "What's the kid's name?" "How old are you, son?" "Where do you go to school?" "What gave you the idea for Shredderman?" "Did your parents have any idea you were breaking up a spy ring?" "What if they don't catch the other spy?" "Are you afraid for your life?"

The chief was studying one of the images on my camera. "Look here!" he said to Sarge. "I think we can pull a license plate off of this one!" He headed back to the station house with my camera, calling, "Get the kid inside! We've got work to do!"

Sarge stepped up to the podium and said, "I'm sorry, but obviously things are developing at a very rapid rate. We'll keep you apprised as things unfold, and I'm sure Nolan will be happy to tell you more about his escapades as Shredderman when the dust settles." He turned to me and grinned, "Isn't that right, Shredderman?"

I said, "Sure," then stepped closer to the microphones and pointed to Chatty Adams. "Except for her. I'm not going to talk to her."

Some people in the crowd snickered. I heard one say, "He's smart, all right."

I fished the two battery packs out of my backpack and looked right at Chatty. "Missing these?"

She let out a gargly scream, and Roy and her cameraman had to hold her back.

I tossed the batteries on the ground and said, "Next time you think you can call someone a nerd, a geek, a fatso, a brat, or a wannabe Barbie and get away with it, remember the kids from Cedar Valley."

"I didn't call them those names!" she cried, looking around. "I swear, I didn't!"

Sarge led me away from the microphones, but we'd only gone a few steps toward the station door when I heard something amazing.

It started with one voice. A voice I'd recognize anywhere.

Bubba Bixby's.

Then other kids chimed in.

Then adults!

It was getting louder...and louder...and louder!

By the time Sarge and I hit the station door, the whole crowd seemed to be chanting it.

"Shred-der-man! Shred-der-man! Shred-der-man!"

I stood there for a second and just listened.

It was the sweetest sound I'd ever heard.

CHAPTER 21
Shredderman Lives!

They set my mom and dad and Mr. Green free, and boy, were they relieved! And when I told Mr. Green about Bubba and Dr. Voss, he about died laughing. "So she doesn't know?" he finally asked.

"Nope. And we're not telling."

"You and Bubba." He chuckled. "Who'd have guessed."

I laughed, too. "Not me, that's for sure!"

When we were finally done answering questions for the police and the FBI, all the reporters wanted to ask me questions. Dad told me I should give Harry Kane first shot at an interview, so that's what I did.

After all, he'd been pretty nice to us kids.

Of course, my secret identity was shot, but with the news stations talking about the spy ring and Shredderman, I figured I could still put my site to *some* use.

First I posted all the pictures I had of the spy guy, with a caption:

IF YOU SEE THIS MAN, CALL THE FBI. HE'S AN ENEMY SPY!

I also put up the movie clip I'd taken of Chatty Adams calling us names.

Thought she could deny it, huh?

Ha!

I sent an e-mail with the **Shredderman** link to an executive at her network, and wrote:

This is why your station didn't get the story.

> **Yours in Truth and Justice,**
> **Shredderman**

We haven't seen Chatty Adams on the air since.

But even though I still had the site, it wasn't like there really was a Shredderman anymore.

Shredderman was...over.

I didn't really miss it at first. I was too busy! The FBI came over and wiped the secret document scans out of my computer.

FBI guys are quick on the computer. Wow!

Then they kept someone posted at our house because they thought the spy guy might come looking for me.

But two days later, a fourth-grade girl spotted the spy guy at a gas station in New Mexico. She'd recognized him from pictures she'd seen on my Web site and called the FBI!

How cool is that!

But mostly I didn't miss having a secret identity because people at school seemed to like my *real* identity. Kids greeted me with, "Hi, Nolan," and "Hey, Shredderman," and "Dude, you rock!" Everyone was saying how cool I was!

Mom worried that kids were just being nice to me because I was now an official celebrity, but I could tell which ones were kissing up to me and which ones were finally just seeing me for me.

I'm no dummy!

So for the first time in my life, I had people to hang around with at school. People to do assignments with. People to eat lunch with!

Having friends is *fun*.

But after about a week it started to sink in— Shredderman was toast.

History.

I'd never be able to wear the mask again.

Mom told me I'd find other ways to fight for truth and justice, but boy, doing it as Shredderman had been so exciting! It made me sad to think that it was over.

Then, one day after school, I was clicking through my site, thinking that it was really time to tear it all down, when my speakers chimed.

I had e-mail.

I clicked on the in-box tab.

It was a message from *Shredderman2*.

At first I was confused. Had I accidentally sent myself an e-mail? I opened it and read:

Yo, Shredderman! You've been an inspiration, man! Check out my site!

Shredderman2.com

> *Yours in Truth and Justice,*
> *Shredderman2*

I couldn't believe my eyes.

Shredderman-*Two*?

Cool!

I clicked on the site. There were only a few pages, but still, it was awesome! The guy had caught someone selling cigarettes in his school's bathroom. Now their dirty deeds were posted on the World Wide Web.

Oh, yeah!

I wrote him back right away—*"Shred on, Shredderman2! Awesome!"*—but just as I sent the message, my speakers chimed again.

More mail.

I blinked at my screen. The new message was from *Shredderdude*.

Shredderdude? Cool!

Over the next few weeks, I got messages from kids shredding on bad guys all over the globe! A kid in England was *ShreddermanUK*. Someone in Australia was *ShredderAussie*. There was a *ShreddermanNY*, a *SeñorShredder*, and then

*Shredderman*3, and *4,* and *5,* and *6* . . . the numbers kept going up!

Girls got into it, too. There were Shreddergirls and Shredderchicks and Shredder*babes* . . . that was kind of embarrassing, but they all wanted the same thing: to help fight for truth and justice.

They also wanted information!

How did I get such close-up shots?

How did I convert my backpack?

What kind of camera did I use?

So I told them everything I could. I gave them ideas! Advice! I told them about my adventures!

And they told me what they were up to, and why!

I felt like I was helping shred on bad guys all over the world!

Way back when *no* one knew my secret identity, Mr. Green told our class that the beauty of Shredderman was that he could be *any*one. He could be the person next to you, the person across the room from you, the person at your bus stop...anyone.

And now I know that what he said is true. Shredderman used to be me, but now it's kids I've

never met, all over the globe! And who knows? Maybe things will come full circle and the next Shredderman will appear at my school.

Or yours!

As long as there are kids who are willing to fight for truth and justice, it'll never be curtains for Shredderman.

So boot up your computer!

Strap on the mask!

Inside all of us, Shredderman lives!

It's a Byrd, it's a Nerd, No... It's

SHREDDERMAN!